GREGORY COOL

CAROLINE BINCH

FRANCES LINCOLN

"Gregory, you *just* like your photos," cried Granny. "It's your Granny got to kiss you at last, an' here's your Grandpa!"

"My, we so pleased to have you home," Grandpa said.

Sitting in the taxi from the airport, squashed tightly between his grandparents, Gregory wished he was back home with his mum and dad. Why did he have to come to Tobago?

The air was stifling and the strange smells disturbed him. Gregory shut his eyes. All of a sudden he felt very tired.

The taxi stopped outside
a very small house.

"Do you really live here?"
asked Gregory. Granny and
Grandpa just laughed as they
took him inside and showed
him his room.

The last he saw before he
fell asleep was a lizard
looking down at him
from the ceiling.

Gregory woke up next morning with just a sheet over him. It was hot! Sun poured in through the open window. There were no toys, no books, no carpet – not even a proper door. Gregory scratched at his arm. Something had bitten him during the night. Was he really expected to stay here for four weeks?

In the kitchen, Granny was cooking breakfast and Grandpa sat at a small table with a boy Gregory hadn't seen before. This must be his cousin. His mum had told him about Lennox, and how he lived with Granny and Grandpa.

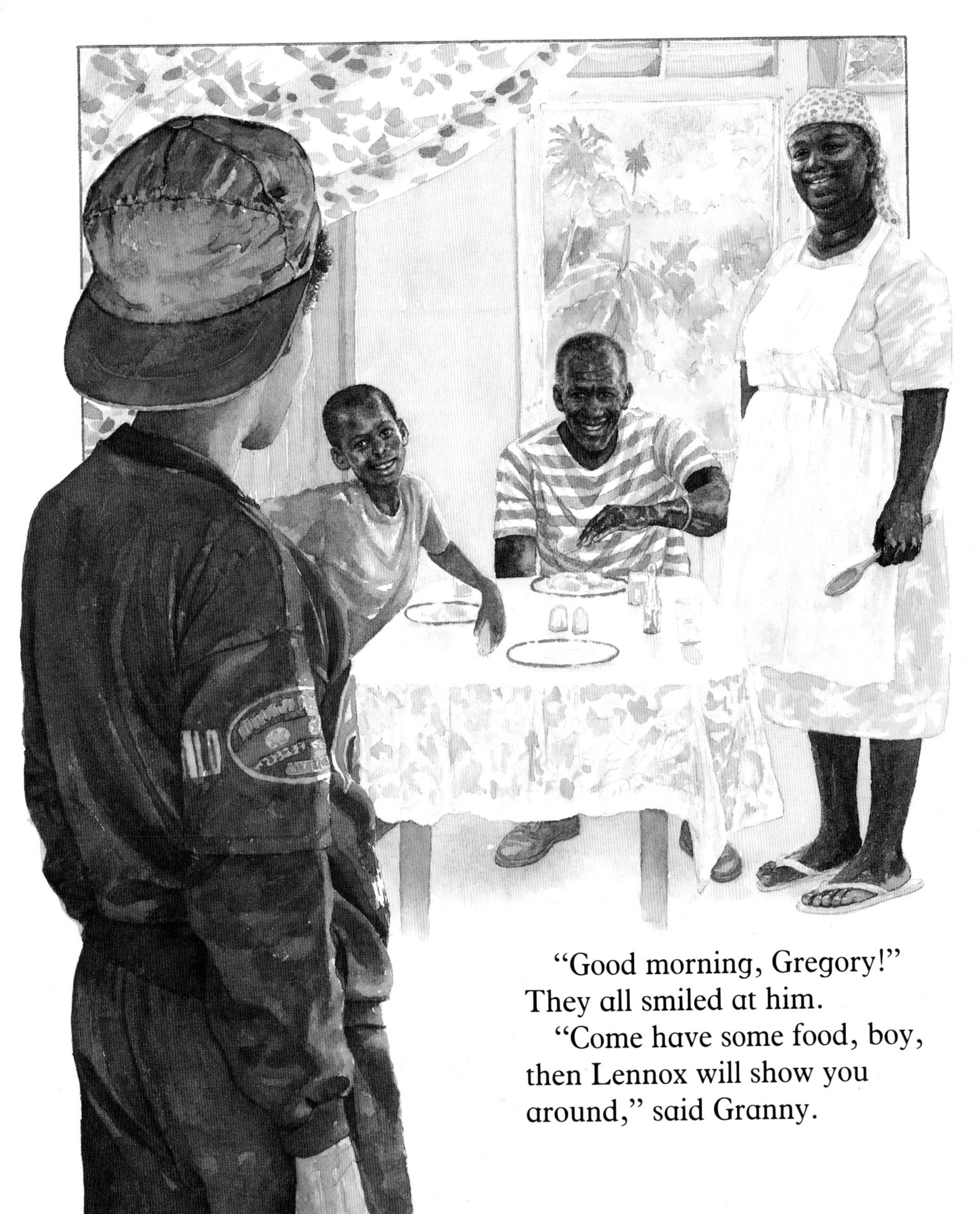

"Good morning, Gregory!" They all smiled at him.

"Come have some food, boy, then Lennox will show you around," said Granny.

Gregory sat down and looked at his breakfast plate. Scrambled eggs – he could deal with that. But it wasn't eggs . . . Gregory spluttered, and spat out the salty stuff as politely as he could.

"Heh, you don't like your bake and buljol?" said Grandpa. "It's just bread and saltfish."

"It's cool," said Gregory. "I'm just not hungry." He drank a glass of fruit juice and followed Lennox outside. Lennox was a year older than Gregory, but much smaller.

"What do you do around here?" asked Gregory. "Got a bike?"

Lennox grinned shyly at him. He had bare feet – Gregory looked at them, then looked away quickly.

AMERICAN
TOURS

"Come, I'll show you the river," said Lennox.

The air was shimmering hot. Gregory sat down in the shade. "I'd rather stay here," he said. "It's cool."

"Well, I go feed the goats, then dip in the river," said Lennox, and off he ran.

Gregory watched him go. Didn't want to play with him anyway, he thought. How can he move so fast in this heat?

He stretched out flat, and dreamed of hamburgers. But supper that evening turned out to be meat so hot and spicy, he could only eat the rice on his plate.

The next day was worse – even hotter, more itchy insect bites, and still nothing to do, not even TV to watch. Gregory thought about going to feed the goats with Lennox, but changed his mind. He wouldn't know how. So instead he sat in the yard and played with his pocket video game until Lennox came back.

He offered Lennox a game.

"Man, this is boss," laughed Lennox.

"You're letting them kill you," said Gregory. "Let me show you." But Lennox jumped up and left, saying, "You sure know it all, Gregory. You sure think you cool."

Granny appeared, carrying a big basket.

"Right now, children," she said, "Grandpa an' me is taking you for a sea-bath."

"Wicked!" shouted Lennox, leaping around the yard.

"Cool," said Gregory politely. Cool was the last thing he felt, but he wasn't going to say so. At least he might get a fizzy drink and an ice-lolly at the beach.

The bus they caught was like an oven, crammed with people. When they finally got there, the beach had palm trees and sand, just like a travel poster. But there wasn't anywhere to get ice-cream or chips – and Gregory had missed out again on breakfast, so he was feeling very hungry.

Lennox rushed off, cartwheeling along the sand.
Gregory sauntered after him. What was there
to get excited about?

The sea looked warm, blue and a bit rough. Gregory was a good swimmer and he jumped into the waves with a shout.

Suddenly, something he saw made him freeze. Sharks! He started swimming for his life. When he reached the shore he was spluttering and shaking with fright.

“Sharks? Oh no, Gregory, they’re not sharks,” said Granny comfortingly, “they’re dolphins. Look see, the dolphin is our best sea-friend.”

Grandpa was chuckling. Lennox fell about laughing. “You a fool, Gregory. You no cool.”

Gregory stomped off. The sun blazed overhead, and
the sand was so hot under his bare feet that he had to run.
Two fishermen called him over, opened a coconut and
offered him a drink.

"Cool," said Gregory. "Thanks."
"Heh," one of them said, "what's your name?"
"Gregory," he told them. "I'm staying with my Granny and Grandpa."
"What you doin' with yourself, then? You been swimming?"
"Yeah," said Gregory. "I thought I saw some sharks, but they were just dolphins, so it was cool."
"Friendly sharks, heh! You got to watch them," they said, grinning. Gregory couldn't help smiling too.
One of the fishermen wrapped a big red fish in a leaf.
"Here, Gregory Cool, take this to your Granny. An' come out fishing with us soon."

Gregory was grinning
when he presented
his parcel to Granny.
"My, what a lovely fish,
Gregory," said Granny,
giving him a hug.
"Tonight we have a big
fish-fry. Now sit down
and eat something, boy."

The picnic was fried chicken, sweet bread, fruit and biscuits. It tasted good. By now, Gregory was feeling thirsty again.

"Got any coconut to drink?" he asked.

"Easy," said Lennox.

He went straight up a coconut tree, no trouble at all. It did look easy, but when Gregory tried, the trunk was far too tall and smooth for him to climb.

Grandpa took one of the young coconuts Lennox had brought down and opened it with his machete. It was full of juice.

"Mmm . . ." said Gregory, drinking it in one gulp.

Suddenly he felt like swimming.

"Hey Lennox, I'm a shark," he said.

"Yeah!" shouted Lennox. "And I'm a massive sting-ray."

The boys jumped into the water together.

Dusk fell. Back at Granny's house, Lennox took Gregory up the hill to watch the moon rise. Gregory kicked off his trainers. He wanted to be barefoot too.

Below them, the lights came on one by one in the small wooden houses. People called to each other. Music played on a radio and someone started to sing. Insects whirred, dogs barked and a donkey brayed.

"Look at the candle-flies," said Lennox, and Gregory noticed tiny lights moving all around them.

Gregory smiled to himself. Drinks from trees. Friendly sharks. A great new cousin. Maybe Tobago was going to be all right after all!

Granny called up from the house below, “Gregory! Lennox! Food ready.”

“OK,” said Gregory. “Cool Greg an’ the Mighty Lennox, we comin’.” Granny laughed and, as they raced down the track together, Lennox shouted, “Yes, you cool, Gregory – you really cool!”

MORE PICTURE BOOKS IN PAPERBACK FROM FRANCES LINCOLN

AMAZING GRACE

Mary Hoffman

Illustrated by Caroline Binch

This award-winning, best-selling picture book tells the story of a young girl, Grace, who wants to play Peter Pan. Her classmates say that Peter was a boy, and besides, he wasn't black... Grace's family say, "You can be anything you want". And in the end Grace makes an amazing Peter Pan.

Highly commended for the Kate Greenaway Medal.

Suitable for National Curriculum, English, Reading, Level 2

(Scottish Guidelines, Level A)

ISBN 0-7112-0699-6 £3.99

THE FIRE CHILDREN

Eric Maddern

Illustrated by Frané Lessac

This intriguing West African creation myth tells how the first spirit-people solve their loneliness using clay and fire - and fill the Earth with children of every colour under the sun!

Suitable for National Curriculum, English, Reading, Level 3

(Scottish Guidelines, Level C)

ISBN 0-7112-0885-9 £3.99

THE SNOWCHILD

Debi Gliori

Poor left-out Katie doesn't know how to play! She has lots of good ideas - but she's always out of step with the other children's games. Then one winter's morning, Katie wakes up and decides to build a snowman...

Suitable for National Curriculum, English, Reading, Level 2

(Scottish Guidelines, Level A)

ISBN 0-7112-0894-8 £3.99

All these books are available at your local bookshop or newsagent, or by post from:

Frances Lincoln Paperbacks, P.O. Box 11, Falmouth, Cornwall.

To order, send:
Title, author, ISBN number and price for each book ordered.
Your full name and address.
Cheque or postal order for the total amount, plus postage and packing.
UK: 80p for the first book, plus 20p for each additional book.
Overseas including Eire: £1.60 for the first book, plus £1.00 for the second book, and 30p for each additional book ordered.

Prices and availability subject to change without notice.

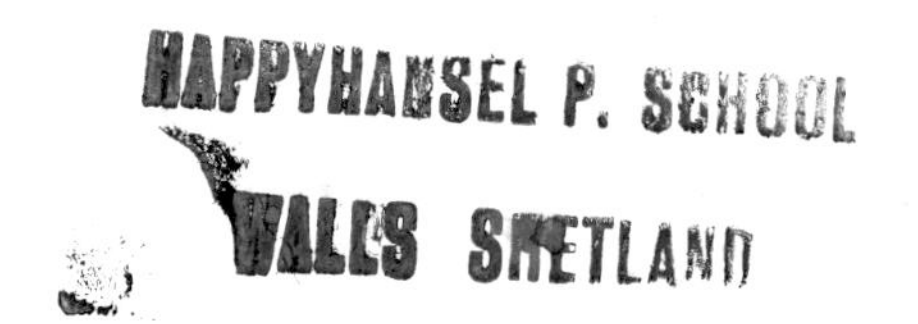

Caroline Binch studied graphic design at Salford Technical College. She has been described by *The Guardian* as "a superb artist, specialising in portraying a vivaciously heightened reality that we can all recognise." *Amazing Grace*, her first book for Frances Lincoln, written by Mary Hoffman, was shortlisted for the Sheffield and Nottinghamshire Children's Book Awards, chosen for Child Education's Best Books of 1991 and Children's Books of the Year 1992, and commended for the Kate Greenaway Medal. In 1993 her book *Hue Boy*, written by Rita Phillips Mitchell and published by Victor Gollancz, won the Smarties Prize.

Caroline lives near Penzance, in Cornwall.